Clifford

TIME FOR SCHOOL

by Gail Herman
Illustrated by Jim Durk
Based on the Scholastic book series
"Clifford The Big Red Dog"
by Norman Bridwell

0-439-66762-3

10 9 8 7 6 5 4 3 2 1   04 05 06 07 08

Printed in the U.S.A.
First printing, September 2004

SCHOLASTIC INC.

New York   Toronto   London   Auckland   Sydney
Mexico City   New Delhi   Hong Kong   Buenos Aires

The sun was shining.

It was the first morning

of summer vacation.

Clifford smiled.

He was going to have a great day
with Emily Elizabeth.

"What should we do today?"

asked Emily Elizabeth.

"Go to the beach?

Play in the park?

Explore Birdwell Island?"

"*Woof!*" barked Clifford.

Emily Elizabeth laughed.

"Good! We'll do it all!"

First they flew a kite

in the park.

"Uh-oh!" said Emily Elizabeth.

"It's stuck."

Clifford bumped the kite

with his nose.

The kite fell out of the tree.

"You're the best, Clifford!"

said Emily Elizabeth.

Next they went to the beach.

It was very windy.

Sand flew everywhere.

Jetta and Mac ran over.

Everyone hid behind Clifford.

"You make a great wind shield!"

said Emily Elizabeth.

The wind calmed down.

Emily Elizabeth and Clifford

went exploring.

They looked in the store windows downtown.

They hiked around the lighthouse.

"We saw the whole island!"

said Emily Elizabeth.

Clifford helped her onto his back.

"Thanks for the ride home,"

said Emily Elizabeth sleepily.

"You're my best friend, Clifford."

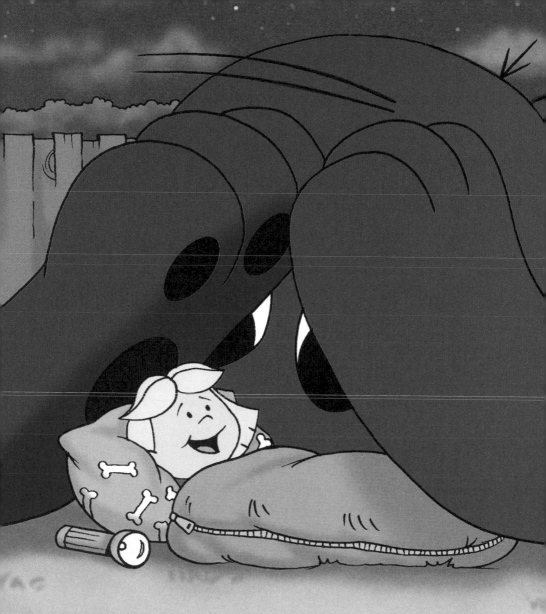

That night, they camped out

in the backyard.

"Your paws make a great tent,"

said Emily Elizabeth.

Clifford watched fireflies

flicker in the yard.

He felt so happy.

Every day, Clifford

and Emily Elizabeth had fun together.

They played baseball in the park

with their friends.

They splashed around in the ocean

and found shells to take home.

One brisk morning,
Emily Elizabeth said,
"I'm sorry, Clifford.
I can't play today."

"Let's go, Emily Elizabeth,"
said Mrs. Howard.
"We'll buy you new clothes
for school."

Clifford went to the park
with Cleo and T-Bone.

It was fun to play with his friends,

but he missed Emily Elizabeth.

That afternoon,

Emily Elizabeth said,

"I can't go to the beach now.

I need a haircut for school."

Clifford waited for Emily Elizabeth

in the backyard.

They would still have a campout,

wouldn't they?

"I need to go to bed early,"

said Emily Elizabeth.

"I have school tomorrow."

In the morning,

Charley and Jetta ran over.

"The school bus broke down!"

said Charley.

"How will we get to school?"

wailed Jetta.

"No problem," said Emily Elizabeth.

"Clifford, we need you!"

"This is great, Clifford!"
said Emily Elizabeth.
"Can you take us to school
every day?"

"*Woof!*" Clifford barked happily.

Summer vacation was over.

But going to school was fun, too!

Do You Remember?

Circle the right answer.

1. Where did Clifford and Emily Elizabeth fly a kite?

    a. At the beach
    b. At school
    c. At the park

2. What did Jetta have with her at the beach?
    a. A telephone
    b. An umbrella
    c. A picnic basket

Which happened first?
Which happened next?
Which happened last?
Write a 1, 2, or 3 in the space after each sentence.

Emily Elizabeth picked up shells. _____

The school bus broke down. _____

Clifford watched fireflies. _____

Answers:

Clifford watched fireflies. (1)
The school bus broke down. (3)
Emily Elizabeth picked up shells. (2)
2. b
1. c